This book belongs to a little chick called:

Isla

Your name goes here

For Joseph from Mummy. GC

To my sister, Alia, who will always
be my little sister. DC

4 North Parade | Bath UK | BA1 1LF
+44(0) 1225 310107
www.nppbooks.co.uk

The Only Penguin

Written by Gemma Cary
Illustrated by Delia Ciccarelli

Bo lived in his icy home with Mama and Papa. They were a happy little family, but sometimes Bo felt lonely, especially when his parents went on one of their long fishing trips.

"I wish I weren't an only penguin," thought Bo.

Bo's friends often talked about their older brothers and sisters.

"My brother taught me how to skate."

"My stepsister took me to the Ice Hole."

"My half brother saved me from a leopard seal!"

"WOW..." said Bo.

"Why don't I have a big brother?" Bo asked his parents.

"Because you were our first chick," Mama replied. "And that makes you very special."

"But I don't want to be an only penguin," said Bo.

"Oh," said Papa. "Well, you'll have to wait until next winter to see if Mama lays an egg."

So Bo waited. When his friends left home to make their journey to the sea, Bo stayed behind.

"**I want to see the new egg**," Bo explained.

And he watched as his friends waddled off to find new adventures.

Winter arrived and so did an egg. Papa proudly
stored the egg in his special pouch to keep it warm,
while Bo went off to share the exciting news.

"I'm going to have a little brother!"
Bo told his neighbours.

"I'm going to have a little brother!"
he told his teacher.

One day, a tiny beak pecked through the egg's shell. A baby chick soon appeared.

"**You have a sister**!" Papa said to Bo.

"Oh," said Bo. "A sister."

"Let's call her Layla," said Papa.

Bo wasn't an only penguin any more. And he soon realised that Layla needed a lot of attention. When they weren't warming Layla with long cuddles, Mama and Papa took turns going fishing to catch food for her.

Bo decided he was big enough to catch his own fish, and he knew just where to go.

Bo had learned about the Ice Hole at school. The stories about it made his feathers shake.

Bo shuffled up to the edge and peered down, watching. He was waiting to spot the grey nose of a hungry leopard seal.

When no nose appeared, Bo bravely slipped into the water for the very first time.

Swimming was like skating super fast – only better!

"This is amazing!" thought Bo.

He dived and looped and glided, catching fish after fish, until he could eat no more.

Suddenly, Bo remembered his family.
Mama and Papa were working hard to
look after Layla while he was busy filling
his own tummy.

Perhaps Bo could do something to help....

Bo swam around looking for the
biggest fish he could find, and –
SNAP! He caught it in his beak.

Even though the fish was really, really heavy, and Bo was really, really tired, he managed to carry it all the way home. He felt happier than ever to see his family!

Bo put down the fish and let out a humungous yawn.

Soon, Layla's little head appeared between Papa's feet.

She smiled up at Bo, then started tucking into the juicy fish.

"**What a helpful big brother**!" said Papa, putting a wing around Bo.

And for the first time, Bo realised that having a little sister meant that he was the big brother. He was the one who could take Layla places and teach her things...and save her from leopard seals!

Being a big brother was going to be **AWESOME**.

Goodbye, Bo!